Will You Forgive Me?

For Oliver and Georgia May – S.G.

For Jane C – P.D.

KINGFISHER
An imprint of Kingfisher Publications Plc
New Penderel House, 283-288 High Holborn
London WC1V 7HZ

First published by Kingfisher 2001
2 4 6 8 10 9 7 5 3 1
1TR/0401/TWP/GC/170MA

Text copyright © Sally Grindley 2001
Illustrations copyright © Penny Dann 2001

A CIP catalogue record for this book
is available from the British Library.

ISBN 0 7534 0474 5

Printed in Singapore

Will You Forgive Me?

Sally Grindley
Illustrated by Penny Dann

KINGFISHER

Jefferson Bear was up a tree eating honey.
    "Save some for our midnight feast, JB,"
called Figgy Twosocks.

Just then, Figgy's brothers pranced by.
"Hey, look at this knobbly stick!"
said Big Smudge.

"That's JB's tickling stick," cried Figgy.
"Put it down. You might break it."

"Scaredy-cat!" jeered Big Smudge,
and he threw the stick in the air.

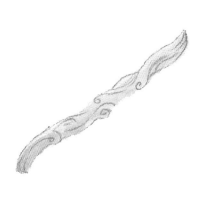

Floppylugs threw
it higher still.

"Bet Figgy can't even throw," he sneered.

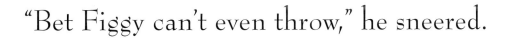

"Bet I can," said Figgy Twosocks crossly.
She grabbed the stick . . .

and threw it.

Up, up, up it went . . .

"OUCH!"

It hit Jefferson Bear on the head.

Then Big Smudge caught the stick. "Let's hide it," he said, and the brothers ran off, sniggering.

Jefferson Bear scrambled down.
"Something hit me on the head,"
he said to Figgy Twosocks.
"Did it?" whispered Figgy.
"Yes, it did," growled Jefferson Bear.
"Now, what I need is a jolly good
scratch. Where's my tickling stick?"

Figgy looked at the ground. "I don't know, JB," she said, and her ears went pink and her nose went all twitchy.

"Well I shall be very cross if it doesn't turn up," said Jefferson Bear, looking at Figgy closely.

Figgy Twosocks rushed off to look for the stick.

She looked in her brothers' den . . .

She looked all along the river bank . . .

She looked in the hollow tree . . .

"What's the matter, Figgy Twosocks?" cried a voice.

It was Hoptail.

"JB's lost his tickling stick, and it's all my fault," said Figgy. "I must find it!"

"Won't any old stick do?" asked Hoptail.

"No," said Figgy. "It's JB's favourite. It's got bumps and knobbles in all the right places, he says."

"Perhaps you should tell Jefferson Bear
what happened," said Hoptail, gently.
    "Then he won't be my friend any more and
we won't have our midnight feast," wailed Figgy.

Figgy Twosocks trudged
through the woods.

"BOO!"

Figgy spun round and saw Jefferson Bear scratching his back against a tree.

"I just can't get to all the little places without my tickling stick," he grumbled.

Figgy felt her ears begin to blush
and her nose begin to twitch.
She didn't like that feeling.
She wanted to tell JB
what had happened.

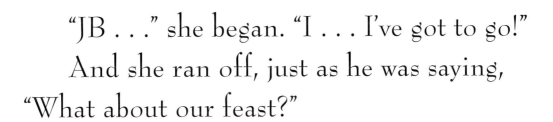

"JB . . ." she began. "I . . . I've got to go!"
And she ran off, just as he was saying,
"What about our feast?"

Figgy ran and ran . . .

and bumped into Buncle the badger.

"Watch out!" grumbled Buncle.
"Sorry," said Figgy. Then she saw
that Buncle was carrying a knobbly stick.

"You've found it!" she cried
excitedly.
"Found what?" said Buncle.
"JB's tickling stick," said Figgy.

"*My* walking stick," said Buncle.
"I found it in my set. Finders keepers."
"But I need it!" pleaded Figgy.

"Well, I might swap it for something," said
Buncle. "Mmm, yes . . . what about some honey?"

"Where will I find honey?" cried Figgy.
Then she remembered Jefferson Bear's tree.

Figgy Twosocks was terrified of climbing trees.

"I've got to do it," she said to herself. "If I don't get his stick back, JB will never forgive me."

She began to climb.
Up and up she went
- her knees began to
knock.

Higher and higher - her
head began to feel funny.

She saw the bees' nest
just above her.

She saw the ground
way down below her.

"Ooo-er," she wailed.
"I don't like this!"
She stretched out
a paw and . . .

WHOOPS!

knocked some honeycomb to the ground.

A bee stung her
angrily on the nose.

"Ouch!"

Then Figgy found she was stuck.
"Help!" she cried. "I'm stuck!"

But nobody heard.

Jefferson Bear was going home that night when he heard someone whimpering.

"Help! Help! Help! Help!"

"Is that you, Figgy?" he called.

"Please help me down, JB," said Figgy.

As soon as she reached the ground, she took some honeycomb and ran off to find Buncle. "Wait there, JB!" she called.

Figgy Twosocks ran back, carrying the tickling stick.

"You've found it!" exclaimed Jefferson Bear.

Figgy's nose began to twitch.

"Figgy," said JB, "your nose is going all twitchy again. Is there something you want to tell me?"

Figgy Twosocks told JB everything.

"I was too scared to tell you before," she whispered.

"Too scared to tell your friend, but not too scared to climb a tree," said Jefferson Bear.

"I'm sorry, JB," said Figgy. "Will you forgive me?"

"I forgive you," said Jefferson Bear.
"Now, let's have that midnight feast."